Moon
Lore

Edited by JOHN MILLER
and TIM SMITH

CHRONICLE BOOKS

SAN FRANCISCO

Printed in Singapore.

Library of Congress Cataloging-in-Publication Data:
Moon lore / edited by John Miller & Tim Smith
p.   cm.
ISBN 0-8118-1104-2
I. Moon—Literary collections.
I. Miller, John, 1959-   . II. Smith, Tim, 1962-
PN6071.M6M666 1995
808.8' 036—dc20   95-12955
CIP

Editing and design: Big Fish Books
Composition: Jennifer Petersen, Big Fish Books

Distributed in Canada by Raincoast Books,
8680 Cambie Street, Vancouver, B.C. V6P 6M9

10 9 8 7 6 5 4 3 2 1

Chronicle Books
275 Fifth Street
San Francisco, CA 94103

THANKS TO

KIRSTEN MILLER

SHELLEY BERNIKER

Contents

Prayer to the Moon

Ho, my hand is this

I shoot a springbok with my hand

By an arrow

I lie down

I will early kill a springbok

Tomorrow

Ho Moon lying there

Let me kill a springbok

Tomorrow

Let me eat a springbok;

With this arrow

Let me shoot a springbok

With this arrow;

Let me eat a springbok

Let me eat filling my body

In the night which is here

Let me fill my body.

Ho Moon lying there

I kill an ostrich tomorrow

With this arrow.

Ho Moon lying there.

Thou must look at this arrow

That I may shoot a springbok with it

tomorrow.

Moon Eclipse Exorcism

*C*ome out come out come out

the moon has been killed

Who kills the moon? crow

who often kills the moon? eagle

who usually kills the moon?

chicken hawk

who also kills the moon? owl

in their numbers they assemble

for moonkilling

come out, throw sticks at your houses

come out, turn your buckets over

spill out all the water don't let it turn

bloody yellow

from the wounding and death

of the moon

.

o what will become of the world, the moon

never dies without cause

only when a rich man is about to be killed

is the moon murdered

look all around the world,

dance, throw your sticks,

  help out,

look at the moon,

  dark as it is now, even if it disappears

it will come back, think of nothing

I'm going back into the house

  and the others went back

          —English translation by Armand Schwerner

The Distance of the Moon

At one time, *according to Sir George H. Darwin, the Moon was very close to the Earth. Then the tides gradually pushed her far away: the tides that the Moon herself causes in the Earth's waters, where the Earth slowly loses energy.*

How well I know! — *old Qfwfq cried,* — the rest of you can't remember, but I can. We had her on top of us all the time, that enormous Moon: when she was full—

nights as bright as day, but with a butter-colored
light—it looked as if she were going to crush us; when
she was new, she rolled around the sky like a black
umbrella blown by the wind; and when she was waxing,
she came forward with her horns so low she seemed
about to stick into the peak of a promontory and get
caught there. But the whole business of the Moon's

phases worked in a dif-
ferent way then: because
the distances from the
Sun were different, and
the orbits, and the angle
of something or other, I
forget what; as for
eclipses, with Earth and
Moon stuck together

the way they were, why, we had eclipses every minute: naturally, those two big monsters managed to put each other in the shade constantly, first one, then the other.

Orbit? Oh, elliptical, of course: for a while it would huddle against us and then it would take flight for a while. The tides, when the Moon swung closer, rise so high nobody could hold them back. There were nights when the Moon was full and very, very low, and the tide was so high that the Moon missed a ducking in the sea by a hair's-breadth; well, let's say a few yards anyway. Climb up the Moon? Of course we did. All you had to do was row out to it in a boat and, when you were underneath, prop a ladder against her and scramble up.

The spot where the Moon was lowest, as she went by, was off the Zinc Cliffs. We used to go out with those little rowboats they had in those days,

round and flat, made of cork. They held quite a few
of us: me, Captain Vhd Vhd, his wife, my deaf cousin,
and sometimes little Xlthlx—she was twelve or so at
the time. On those nights the water was very calm, so
silvery it looked like mercury, and the fish in it, violet-
colored, unable to resist the Moon's attraction, rose to
the surface, all of them, and so did the octopuses and
the saffron medusas. There was always a flight of tiny
creatures—little crabs, squid, and even some weeds,
light and filmy, and coral plants—that broke from the
sea and ended up on the Moon, hanging down from
that lime-white ceiling, or else they stayed in midair, a
phosphorescent swarm we had to drive off, waving
banana leaves at them.

This is how we did the job: in the boat we had
a ladder: one of us held it, another climbed to the top,

and a third, at the oars, rowed until we were right under the moon: that's why there had to be so many of us (I only mentioned the main ones). The man at the top of the ladder, as the boat approached the Moon, would become scared and start shouting: "Stop! Stop! I'm going to bang my head!" That was the impression you had, seeing her on top of you, immense, and all rough with sharp spikes and jagged, saw-tooth edges. It may be different now, but then the Moon, or rather the bottom, the underbelly of the Moon, the part that passed closest to the earth and almost scraped it, was covered with a crust of sharp scales. It had come to resemble the belly of a fish, and the smell too, as I recall, if not downright fishy, was faintly similar, like smoked salmon.

In reality, from the top of the ladder, standing erect on the last rung, you could just touch the

Moon if you held your arms up. We had taken the measurements carefully (we didn't yet suspect that she was moving away from us); the only thing you had to be careful about was where you put your hands. I always chose a scale that seemed fast (we climbed in groups of five or six at a time), then I would cling first with one hand, then with both, and immediately I would feel ladder and boat drifting away from below me, and the motion of the Moon would tear me from the Earth's attraction. Yes, the Moon was so strong that she pulled you up; you realized this the moment you passed from one to the other: You had to swing up abruptly, with a kind of somersault, grabbing the scales, throwing your legs over your head, until your feet were on the Moon's surface. Seen from the Earth, you looked as if you were hanging there with your head down, but for you, it was the normal position, and the only odd thing was that when you raised your eyes you saw the sea above you, glistening, with the boat and the others upside down, hanging like a bunch of grapes from the vine.

—*Translated by William Weaver*

Marcu Beza

Romanian Moon Incantations

A new moon has put on a crown of precious gems. Luminous moon, who art in heaven and seest everything on the earth, I find no rest in my home from the hatred of my enemies who have risen up with great wickedness against me and against my house; and thou too, bright moon, shalt have no peace either, unless thou takest the spell and charm from our house, and from our table, and from my face, and from the face of my wife, and from our property, and from our wealth. Luminous moon, whether the spell has been cast by a man or by a woman or by a youth, take the spell from our house and from my wealth and from my cattle, and from my garden, and from my orchard, and from all my things! . . ."

"O luminous moon, luminous moon, come and take away the spell and the desolation, and the hatred from the world, and from my house, and from my table, and from my garden, and from my vineyard, and from my craft, and from my trade, and from my

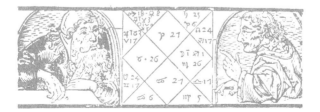

purse, and drive it away to wild mountains and forests; and us and our children and those who shall be born unto us hereafter, leave us clean and pure like refined gold and like the sun that shines brilliantly in the skies!"

Moon Prayer

Monostatos.

Ah, here I find the timid maiden.

The flame which in me burns will

consume me.

(He looks around.)

If I only knew whether I am alone and

no one listening. A little kiss, I should

think, would be excusable.

Love in every heart is reigning,

Bills and coos, caresses and embraces,

But my love she is disdaining

 Just because my skin is brown.

Have I not a heart within me?

Why should maidens at me frown?

Without wife ever to dwell,

Is worse than the fire of hell.

Therefore will I while I live,

Bill and kiss and tender be.

Dear good moon, forgive, forgive,

 A white maid has enticed me.

White is lovely, I must kiss.

Moon, oh hide thyself the while,

And if it disturbs thy bliss,

Close thine eyes, and take it not amiss.

Denise Levertov

Secret Festival;
September Moon

Pandemonium of owls

plying from east to west and

west to east, over the full-moon sea of

mown grass.

The low-voiced

and the wailing high-voiced

hooting together, neither in dialogue

nor in unison,

an overlapping

antiphonal a fox

barks to,

as if to excel, whose obligato

the owls ignore.

They raise

the roof of the dark; ferocious

their joy in the extreme silver

the moon has floated out from itself,

luminous air in which their eyes

don't hurt or close,

the night of the year

their incantations have raised—

and if

foxes believe it's theirs, there's enough to slip

over and round them, earthlings, of owlish fire.

Your Moon Sign

QUICK CLUES TO THE NATAL SIGNS AND HOUSES

This is a very brief outline which you can use to jog your memory. This just gives the impact of each sign on the inner personality.

ARIES (FIRST) Lively, positive personality. Enthusiastic, self-motivated and outgoing but lacking in patience and consideration for others.

TAURUS (SECOND) Steady type, sorts out what is valuable to him and then hangs on to it. Family person, sensual, and musical. Resourceful and materialistic.

GEMINI (THIRD) Communicator, teacher, salesman or travel agent. Usually found on the phone; needs to keep up to date. Mental activity needed; versatile and easily bored.

CANCER (FOURTH) Needs a home base and family around. Good to others but will lean on them. Moody; wants a quiet life. Enjoys travel, novelty. Needs personal security.

LEO (FIFTH) Youthful and playful, loyal but dogmatic. Needs to be respected by others. Hard workers especially in a creative field. Likes children.

VIRGO (SIXTH) Shy, inward-looking type, dedicated worker, perfectionist. Likes to help others but moans about it. Businesslike, discriminating. Apparently cool emotionally; has strong but contained feelings.

LIBRA (SEVENTH) Ambitious, determined, also loving. Needs to be surrounded by beauty. Theorizer; may have difficulty putting ideas into practice. Needs partners and companions to complement self and achieve harmony.

SCORPIO (EIGHTH) Steady, reliable workers. Determined and independent. Strong, intense but restrained personality. Quick to anger but very caring to those who matter. Can transform self and others.

SAGITTARIUS (NINTH) Restless, but also needing a secure base. Philosophic and broad-minded. Interested in sport, culture and all wide ideas.

CAPRICORN (TENTH) Ambitious, loyal and caring family person. Career important; good business head. Lacking in confidence; shy, kind. Restrained and self-motivated. Seeks position of authority.

AQUARIUS (ELEVENTH) Friendly, humanitarian, politically minded. Needs family but cannot be confined to the home. Serious-minded, eccentric and detached.

PISCES (TWELFTH) Gentle, compassionate, mystical, reclusive. Kind, but can be too self-sacrificing. Religious outlook. Sensitive, vulnerable. Artistic and creative.

●

THE MOON IN THE ASTROLOGICAL HOUSES

The houses are as interesting as the signs, although their impact on a birthchart is different. The signs show *what you are* while the houses show *what you do*. In this section we will look at the Moon in each house position, look a little more closely at the areas of life which each house position represents.

MOON IN THE FIRST HOUSE

You love your home and family and would not be happy to live alone. Your nature may appear quiet and introverted but you have an inner desire to be recognized as a person in your own right. You will do much to help others but you're not prepared to make too many sacrifices on their behalf. Your mother was a strong influence on you and may indeed have been an exceptional woman in *her* own right; you could even find yourself walking in her shadow. The sea calls you so strongly that you may choose to live and work on it. You may be physically restless, finding it hard to sit still; alternatively you could have a love of travel, preferably with your family along for the ride. You may be drawn to hobbies or even work in the field of food and nutrition and could be a vegetarian, possibly due to your love of animals. It comes naturally to you to support the underdog wherever you can. This placement suggests a need to work for the public in some way, either before them as some kind of celebrity or, more likely in some kind of humanitarian or welfare capacity. Being finely tuned in to your own body you usually know if you are going down with some illness. You must try not to allow your moods to dominate your personality.

MOON IN THE SECOND HOUSE
(ACCIDENTAL EXALTATION)

Material matters are important to you and you seem to need the security of money and possessions. There is a suggestion that these may be hard to obtain or to keep hold of in some way. Your need for security may result from a materially or emotionally deprived childhood. There is a shrewd and slightly calculating business head on your shoulders but your pleasant approach to others hides this well. Women will be involved in your personal finances in some way and you could be helped by women, possibly by inheritance or through family connections. You will probably take an interest in Taurean pursuits such as cooking, dancing, building, music, the arts, gardening and the creation of beauty.

MOON IN THE THIRD HOUSE

The Moon here shows the need to communicate, which could lead you towards a career in travel, the media or education. You are restless and curious but possibly lacking in concentration and easily bored. You pick up knowledge casually from others as you go through life. Your parents might be clever and bookish. Throughout life you will keep learning and then passing on information to others. You have a natural affinity to the telephone and also to vehicles which may, to others, look like an obsession.

MOON IN THE FOURTH HOUSE

(ACCIDENTAL DIGNITY)

This is the natural house of the Moon due to its association with the sign of Cancer which is ruled by the Moon. You prefer to work at home or at least to do your own thing, preferably in your own business. You may be nervous of the big wide world and have a habit of scuttling back home when the going gets rough. You are sympathetic towards those who are weak and helpless and are especially fond of animals. You could be strongly attached to your parents or, on the other hand, separated from them by circumstances beyond your control. It is possible that you lack confidence or feel insecure as an adult due to childhood problems; you need love and affection and should try to avoid hurting yourself further by forming relationships with destructive types. The past attracts you and this might lead you to work in the field of antiques or to be a collector of old and valuable objects. You may have a strong urge to live on or near the sea.

MOON IN THE FIFTH HOUSE

You are attracted to the world of children which might draw you to work as an infant school teacher or become involved with young people's sporting activities. Your emotions are strong and you seek fulfillment on both a practical and romantic level in relationships. You could have a number of affairs if marriage does not work out for you. You have a good deal of charm and attractive youthful appearance which is useful to you as you would take naturally to a rather public type of career such as the theater or in marketing and public relations.

Be careful not to be too clinging towards your children.
A creative outlet is an emotional necessity for you. You
would make a good teacher, writer or publisher.

MOON IN THE SIXTH HOUSE

You have a strong urge to serve the needs of others and
may work in some kind of caring professions, especially
medicine. You could be drawn to a career which
involves the production of food and anything which
helps the public to stay in good health. Your career will
have to appeal to you on an emotional level and you
could even walk out of a job if the atmosphere or the
people there didn't suit you. You may be restless and
better suited to having a couple of part-time jobs rather
than one full-time one. You have consideration for others and would yourself be a rather maternal employer.

MOON IN THE SEVENTH HOUSE

You get on with most people because you need company and companionship. Where relationships are
concerned, you will bend over backwards to make them

work but it may be at quite a price. There
is a feeling that while young you are
not quite sure who you are and you
may feel the need to have your personality

and even your opinions validated by others. You prefer
to work in co-operation with a partner or in a small
group and you may be drawn to work in some kind of
caring job like personnel management. You are politically minded and also have a good grasp of office pol-
itics. Glamour appeals to you, drawing you towards the
world of fashion and music, and this could become
part of an interesting hobby for you. Your partner may

be moody and difficult, but it is possible that *you* could understand him or her where others just don't.

MOON IN THE EIGHTH HOUSE

Women will be instrumental in helping you to gain money or prestige in some way. You could work in trades which cater to women's needs or work mainly among women. You have an interest in psychic matters and you will be drawn to the mediumistic and spiritual side of these things. Your clairvoyance could be prodigious but it will depend upon other factors on the chart as to how this is directed. There is a feeling that love, affection, sensuality and sex are important factors in your chart and you could have your greatest successes in life in partnership with someone who inspires you both mentally and sexually. You can be devious, hurtful and destructive, even to the point of destroying your career or your future chances of success if you feel thwarted. Strange position this, as both the Moon and the house are so involved with instinctive and reactive behavior.

MOON IN THE NINTH HOUSE

Religion and philosophy will be an important part of your life and you will have to go on some kind of inward journey in order to find your way forward. You think deeply and will turn to a consideration of the deeper things of life. You are a natural psychic with the ability to see and feel beyond the boundaries of this Earth. Travel will be an important part of your life, as will any dealings with foreigners or foreign goods. You could be a restless roamer who never really touches down for long anywhere; however, you are a natural teacher and instructor of others with a clear view of how to do things. You could find yourself attached to slightly crazy people.

MOON IN THE TENTH HOUSE
(ACCIDENTAL DETRIMENT)

This gives you an inner urge to shine before the public in some way, or to help humanity on a grand scale. There is evidence of an emotionally impoverished childhood during which something went strangely wrong. Your parents (especially your mother) could have been super-achievers whom you seek to emulate. You will change jobs a few times until you find the right road for you. My feelings are that that road will be intensely personal, leading to a good deal of acclaim—or even, if the Moon is badly aspected, public scandal and ruin. You are drawn to a career which seeks to supply the needs of women or which is traditionally carried out by women. Sales, marketing, domestic goods and women's literature are a few possibilities. Your standing in the community, especially your career standing, is of paramount importance to you and even to others who are around you. You will be known and remembered by many before your life is done. To some extent this is a compensation for feelings of insecurity deriving from your difficult childhood, and a somewhat arid personal life, but just keep telling yourself that you will one day make it and, somehow, you will find the strength to carry on.

MOON IN THE ELEVENTH HOUSE

You enjoy the company of others and could be heavily involved in some kind of club or society. Being extremely independent, you hate to be told what to do. Your family are sometimes left in the dark as to your plans and feelings but there is a possibility that you, yourself may find it hard to know what you really *do* feel at times. Your aims in life may change dramatically from time to time due to circumstances. Friends, especially female ones, are very helpful to you, and you have a strange kind of luck that brings them running to you in times of trouble. You are well organized and able to manage others, but you can on occasion misjudge people and be taken advantage of by more astute and crafty types.

MOON IN THE TWELFTH HOUSE

You seek to hide away from the world from time to time and to work in seclusion. Certainly you are happiest doing your own thing and working from your own home. Women will be an important part of any achievement, while men tend to interfere with your life, particularly with your career. You need to get away from time to time to recharge your batteries; too much stress will make you ill. You could be very creative, as you have a rich imagination. Your instinctive need to care for others may lead you to work in the field of nursing or with animals. You may be too ready to sacrifice yourself for others. There is a secret side to your life; you may have to keep the secrets of others.

How the Moon First Came into the Sky

In a certain town there lived Njomm Mbui (juju sheep). He made great friends with Etuk (antelope), whose home was in the bush.

When the two animals grew up they went out and cut farms. Njomm planted plantains in his, while Etuk set his with coco-yams.

When the time came round for the fruits to ripen, Njomm went to his farm and cut a bunch of plantains, while Etuk dug up some of his coco.

Each cleaned his food and put it in the pot to cook. When all was ready they sat down and ate.

Next morning Etuk said to Njomm, "Let us change. I saw a bunch of plantains in your farm which I would like to get. Will you go instead to mine and take some coco?"

This was arranged, and Etuk said to Njomm, "Try to beat up fu-fu." Njomm tried, and found it very good. He gave some to Etuk. The latter ate all he wanted, then book the bunch of plantains and hung it in his house.

Next morning he found that the fruit had grown soft, so he did not care to eat it. He therefore took the plantains and threw them away in the bush.

During the day Mbui came along and smelt plantains. He looked round till he found them, then picked one up and began to eat. They were very sweet. He ate his fill, then went on, and later met a crowd of the Nshum people (apes). To them he said, "Today I found a very sweet thing in the bush."

In course of time Etuk grew hungry again, and Njomm said to him. "If you are hungry, why don't you tell me?"

He went to his farm and got four bunches of plantains. As he came back he met the monkey people. They begged for some of his fruit, so he gave it to them.

After they had eaten all there was, they in turn went on, and met a herd of wild boars (Ngumi). To these they said, "There is very fine food to be got from Njomm and Etuk."

The Ngumi therefore came and questioned Etuk, "Where is coco to be had?" and Etuk answered, "The coco belongs to me."

The boars begged for some, so Etuk took a basket, filled it at his farm, and gave it to them.

After they were satisfied, they went on their way and next morning met Njokk (elephant).

To him they said, "Greetings, Lord! Last night we got very good food from the farms over there."

Njokk at once ran and asked the two friends, "Whence do you get so much food?" They said, "Wait a little."

Njomm took his long machete and went to his farm. He cut five great bunches of plantains and carried them back. Etuk also got five baskets full of coco, which he brought to elephant. After the latter had eaten all this, he thanked them and went away.

All the bush beasts came in turn and begged for food, and to each the two friends gave willingly of all that they had. Lastly also came Mfong (bush cow).

Now not far from the two farms there was a great river called Akarram (The One-Which-Goes-Round). In the midst of it, deep down, dwelt crocodile. One day Mfong went down into the water to drink, and from him crocodile learned that much food was to be had nearby.

On this crocodile came out of the water and began walking towards the farms. He went to Njomm and Etuk and said, "I am dying of hunger, pray give me food."

Etuk said, "To the beasts who are my friends I will give all I have, but to you I will give nothing, for you are no friend of mine;" but Njomm said, "I do not like you very much, yet I will give you one bunch of plantains."

Crocodile took them and said: "Do not close your door tonight when you lie down to sleep. I will come back and buy more food from you at a great price."

He then went back to the water and sought out a python, which dwelt there. To the latter he said:

"I have found two men on land, who have much food." Python said, "I too am hungry. Will you give me to eat?"

So crocodile gave him some of the plantains which he had brought. When python had tasted he said: "How sweet it is! Will you go back again and bring more?" Crocodile said, "Will you give me something with which to buy?" and python answered, "Yes. I will give you something with which you can buy the whole farm."

On this he took from within his head a shining stone and gave it to crocodile. The latter started to go back to the farm. As he went, night fell and all the road grew dark, but he held in his jaws the shining stone, and it made a light on his path, so that all the way was bright. When he neared the dwelling of the two friends he hid the stone and called, "Come out and I will show you something which I have brought."

It was very dark when they came to speak with him. Slowly the crocodile opened his claws, in which he held the stone, and it began to glimmer between them. When he held it right out, the whole place became so bright that one could see to pick up a needle or any small thing. He said, "The price of this that I bring is one whole farm."

Etuk said: "I cannot buy. If I give my farm, nothing remains to me. What is the use of this great shining stone if I starve to death?" But Njomm said: "I will buy—oh, I will buy, for my farm full of plantains, for that which you bring fills the whole earth with light. Come let us go. I will show you my farm. From here to the waterside all round is my farm. Take it all, and do what you choose with it, only give me the great shining stone that, when darkness falls, the whole earth may still be light."

Crocodile said, "I agree."

Then Njomm went to his house with the stone, and Etuk went to his. Njomm placed it above the lintel, that it might shine for all the world; but

Etuk closed his door and lay down to sleep.

In the morning Njomm was very hungry, but he had nothing to eat, because he had sold his farm for the great white stone.

Next night and the night after he slept full of hunger, but on the third morning he went to Etuk and asked, "Will you give me a single coco-yam?" Etuk answered: "I can give you nothing, for now you have nothing to give in exchange. It was not I who told you to buy the shining thing. To give something, when plenty remains, is good; but none but a fool would give his all, that a light may shine in the dark!"

Njomm was very sad. He said: "I have done nothing bad. Formerly no one could see in the night-time. Now the python stone shines so that everyone can see to go wherever he chooses."

All that day Njomm still endured, though nearly dying of hunger, and at nighttime he crept down to the water, very weak and faint.

By the riverside he saw a palm tree, and on it a man trying to cut down clusters of ripe kernels; but this was hard to do, because it had grown very dark.

Njomm said, "Who is there?" and the man answered, "I am Effion Obassi."

The second time Njomm called, "What are you doing?" and Effion replied, "I am trying to gather palm kernels, but I cannot do so, for it is very dark amid these great leaves."

Njomm said to him, "It is useless to try to do such a thing in the dark. Are you blind?"

Effion answered, "I am not blind. Why do you ask?"

Then Njomm said: "Good; if you are not blind, I beg you to throw me down only one or two palm kernels, and in return I will show you a thing more bright and glorious than any you have seen before."

Effion replied: "Wait a minute, and I will try to throw a few down to you. Afterwards you shall show me the shining thing as you said."

He then threw down three palm kernels, which Njomm took, and stayed his hunger a little. The latter then called; "Please try to climb down. We will go together to my house."

Effion tried hard, and after some time he stood safely at the foot of the tree by the side of Njomm.

Soon as they got to his house, Njomm said, "Will you wait here a little while I go to question the townspeople?"

First he went to Etuk and asked: "Will you not give me a single coco to eat? See, the thing which I bought at the price of all that I had turns darkness to light for you, but for me, I die of hunger."

Etuk said: "I will give you nothing. Take back the thing for which you sold your all, and we will stay in our darkness as before."

Then Njomm begged all of the townsfolk that they would give him ever so little food in return for the light he had bought for them. Yet they all refused.

So Njomm went back to his house and took the shining stone, and gave it to Effion Obassi, saying: "I love the earth folk, but they love not me. Now take the shining thing for which I gave my whole possessions. Go back to the place from whence you came, for I know that you belong to the sky people, but when you reach your home in the heavens, hang up my stone in a place where all the earth folk may see its shining, and be glad."

Then Effion took the stone, and went back by the road he had come. He climbed up the palm tree, and the great leaves raised themselves upwards, pointing to the sky, and lifted him, till, from their points, he could climb into heaven.

When he reached his home, he sent and called all the Lords of the Sky and said, "I have brought back a thing today which can shine so that all the earth will be light. From now on everyone on earth or in heaven will be able to see at the darkest hour of the night."

The chiefs looked at the stone and wondered. Then they consulted together, and made a box.

Effion said, "Make it so that the stone can shine out only from one side."

When the box was finished, he set the globe of fire within, and said: "Behold, the stone is mine. From this time all the people must bring me food. I will no longer go to seek any for myself."

For some time they brought him plenty, but after a while they grew tired. Then Effion covered the sides of the box, so that the stone could not shine till they brought him more. That is the reason why the moon is sometimes dark, and people on earth say: "It is the end of the month. The sky people have grown weary of bringing food to Effion Obassi and he will not let his stone shine out till they bring a fresh supply."

Scottish Moon Charms

They have still among them a great number of charms for the cure of different diseases; they are all invocations, perhaps transmitted to them from the times of popery, which increasing knowledge will bring into disuse.

They have opinions, which cannot be ranked with superstition because they regard only natural effects. They expect better crops of grain, by sowing their seeds in the moon's increase. The moon has great influence in vulgar philosophy. In my memory it was a precept annually given in one of the *English* Almanacks, *to kill hogs when the moon was increasing, and the bacon would prove the better in boiling.*

Anonymous

The Amazonian Creation of the Moon

The man cut his throat and left his head there.

The others went to get it.

When they got there they put the head in a sack.

Farther on the head fell out onto the ground.

They put the head back in the sack.

Farther on the head fell out again.

Around the first sack they put a second one that was thicker.

But the head fell out just the same.

It should be explained that they were taking the head

to show to the others.

They did not put the head back in the sack.

They left it in the middle of the road.

They went away.

They crossed the river.

But the head followed them.

They climbed up a tree full of fruit

to see whether it would go past.

The head stopped at the foot of the tree

and asked them for some fruit.

So the men shook the tree.

The head went to get the fruit.

Then it asked for some more.

So the men shook the tree

so that the fruit fell into the water.

The head said it couldn't get the fruit from there.

So the men threw the fruit a long way

to make the head go a long way to get it so they could go.

While the head was getting the fruit

the men got down from the tree and went on.

The head came back and looked at the tree

and didn't see anybody

so went on rolling down the road.

The men had stopped to wait

to see whether the head would follow them.

They saw the head come rolling.

They ran.

They got to their hut they told the others that the head
was rolling after them and to shut the door.

All the huts were closed tight.

When it got there the head commanded them to open
the doors.

The owners would not open them because they were afraid.

So the head started to think what it would turn into.

If it turned into water they would drink it.

If it turned into earth they would walk on it.

 If it turned into a house they
would live in it.

If it turned into a steer they
would kill it and eat it.

If it turned into a cow they would milk it.

If it turned into wheat they would eat it.

If it turned into a bean they would cook it.

If it turned into the sun

when men were cold it would heat them.

If it turned into rain the grass would grow and

the animals would crop it.

So it thought, and it said, "I will turn into the moon."

It called, "Open the doors, I want to get my things."

They would not open them.

The head cried. It called out, "At least give me

my two balls of twine."

They threw out the two balls of twine through a hole.

It took them and threw them into the sky.

It asked them to throw it a little stick too

to roll the thread around so it could climb up.

Then it said, "I can climb, I am going to the sky."

It started to climb.

The men opened the doors right away.

The head went on climbing.

The men shouted, 'You going to the sky, head?"

It didn't answer.

As soon as it got to the Sun

it turned into the Moon.

Toward evening the Moon was white, it was beautiful.

And the men were surprised

to see that the head had turned into the Moon.

—*Translated by W. S. Merwin*

Moon
Haiku

The moon's in mid-heaven;
I wander
Through poor streets.

●

Waning and wasting away
The moon disappears—
How cold a night!

●

The summer moon shines

On transient dreams

In the octopus pot.

●

Over the portal

Ivy creeps—

Evening moon.

●

My shadow in front,

It leads me home—

Moonlight night!

Moon
Gardening

THE MEANINGS OF THE SIGNS
This is an alphabetical listing of crops
and the times which are said to be most
favorable for planting and other chores, according to
the best information we can obtain.

Other signs are said to aid as follows: The
Ram, vines and stalks; the Bull, root crops of quick
growth; Twins, melon seeds—although some
"experts" disagree; Balance, pulp growth and roots;

the Goat, pulp stalk or roots.

Not that Aquarius used to be known as the Butler, is now the Waterman. He's not popular under any name with Moonlore followers.

●

Apples—Pick in the Dark of the Moon to keep
  from rotting.

Artichoke—Plant in the Full of the Moon.

Asparagus—Plant in the Light of the Moon.

Barley—Plant in the Light of the Moon.

Beans—If planted when the horns of the Moon
  are up, will readily pole; but if planted
  when the horns are down, will not. If Cancer comes at Full of Moon, a good time to
  plant beans. Gemini is also a good planting sign.

Beets—Plant from Full Moon to New Moon, in

sign of Pisces.

Broccoli—Plant in the Light of the Moon.

Brussels Sprouts—Plant in the Light of the Moon.

Cabbage—Plant in Full of Moon; for early cabbage,

sign should be in Aries.

Carrots—Plant from New Moon to Full Moon, in

Pisces.

Cauliflower—Plant in the Light of the Moon.

Celery—Plant in the Light of the Moon.

Cereals—When Planted in the waxing of the Moon,

germinate more rapidly than when planted in

waning of the Moon.

Chicory—Plant in Full of Moon

Citrons—Plant in the Full of the Moon.

Corn—Plant in the Light of the Moon; cut in the

Decrease of the Moon else it will spoil. Some
consider Scorpio a good planting sign.

Cress—Plant in the Light of the Moon.

Cucumbers—Plant in the Full of the Moon, in Pisces.

Eggplant—Plant in the Full of the Moon.

Endive—Plant in Light of the Moon.

Kohl Rabi—Plant in the Light of the Moon.

Leek—Plant in Light of Moon.

Lentils—If Cancer comes at Full Moon, a good time
to plant.

Lettuce—Plant in Light of Moon.

Mangel-Wurzel—Plant from Full Moon to New
Moon, in Pisces.

Melon Seeds—Pisces is a good time for planting, in
Light of Moon. Gemini is said to be a good
melon sign.

Muskmelon—Plant in Full Moon.

Oats—Plant in Light of Moon.

Onions—Plant when the horns of the Moon are
     down. Bend over the tops on 7 Sleepers (June
     27) to make them grow large.

Parsley—Plant in Light of the Moon.

Parsnips—Plant from New Moon to Full Moon,
     in Pisces.

Peas—Best time to sow peas is day after New Moon.

Pepper—Plant from Full Moon to 3rd Quarter.

Potatoes—Plant in the Dark or Waning Moon.

Pumpkin—Plant from Full Moon to 3rd Quarter.

Radishes—Plant from New Moon to Full Moon, in
     Pisces.

Rutabaga—Plant from New Moon to Full Moon.

Root Crops—All root crops that produce their yield

in the ground should be planted in the Old

or Decrease of the Moon to produce good

yield. Taurus is a good sign for planting.

Spinach—Plant in the Light of the Moon.

Squash—Plant in the Full of the Moon.

Tomatoes—Plant in the Full of the Moon. Some

farmers prefer Gemini as planting sign.

Turnips—Plant in 3rd Quarter.

Watermelon—Plant in 2nd Quarter. Gemini is a

good planting sign.

SIGNS FOR FARM AND HOUSEHOLD

Pioneers, carrying on traditions of their European homelands, followed these rules in America's early days:

Butcher—Cattle slaughtered in the Fulling of the Moon are said to be fatter and give juicier meat than those butchered in the Waning Moon. If hogs are slaughtered in the Waxing of the Moon, the pork will swell in the barrel.

Boil Soup—Boil soap in the Increase of the Moon.

Building a Rail Fence—Lay the first or lower rail when the horns of the Moon are up; put in the stakes and finish the fence when the horns are down. Set fence posts in the Old of the Moon.

Cut Hair—Cut your hair in the Increase of the
Moon if you want a full head of hair; to thin
it, cut during the Wane.

Cut Timber—Timber cut in the Old of the Moon
will not be eaten by worms nor snap in burning, and will last much longer than if cut at
any other time.

Eradicating Weeds—For best results against noxious
weeks, briars and bushes, cut in the Old of the
Moon, preferably in Leo, Gemini and Virgo.

Fishing—Fish bite best in the signs of the Fish,
Crab or Scorpion. Fish at night in the Light
of the Moon, but not in daytime. During
Dark of Moon, fish in daytime, as fish cannot see in Dark of Moon and are hungrier
in daytime.

Planting Flowers—Plant flowers in the Increase of the Moon, in Cancer or Libra. The Pennsylvania Dutch like to plant in Virgo, "The Posy Lady"; first day her sign appears is said to be the strongest influence for bountiful growth.

Roofing a building—Shingle buildings when the horns of the Moon are down, and the Moon is on the wane, else the shingles will curl up at the edges and the nails will draw out.

Sauer Kraut Making—Best time to make sauer kraut is in the decrease of the Moon. Pisces, a watery sign, is said to be very favorable for sauer kraut.

Shear Sheep—Shear in the Increase of the Moon, and the wool will grow again better and stronger.

Spread Manure—Spread manure when the horns of
the Moon are down.

Transplanting flowers—Best time to transplant flowers is from New Moon to 1st Quarter. Flowers transplanted during Full Moon are said to
bloom double.

Seafood—Crabs, oysters, mussels and snails are
believed to be fattest at Full Moon.

Paul Verlaine

Clair de Lune

Your soul is a sealed garden, and there go
With masque and bergamasque fair com-
panies
Playing on lutes and dancing and as though
Sad under their fantastic fripperies.

Though they in minor keys go carolling
Of love the conqueror and of life the boon
They seem to doubt the happiness they sing
And the song melts into the light of the moon,

The sad light of the
moon, so lovely fair
That all the birds dream
in the leafy shade
And the slim fountains
sob into the air
Among the marble stat-
ues in the glade.

—*Translated by Arthur Symons*

Moon, Moon

I see the moon,

    And the moon sees me;

God bless the moon,

    And God bless me.

Moon, moon,

Mak' me a pair o'shoon,

And I'll dance till you be done.

Pretty, Pretty Moon a Fell Down pon Me

This is a story about a market woman.
Now they used to go to Old Harbour
to market—Old Harbour Bay, from this
place name Point Hill. So this woman was coming. It
was *very* late 'cause market break up and have to walk
on foot—not the days when you have motor vehicles. So when she was coming on, she reach a place
named Florry Bridge, and she see a *duppy*. The duppy
on the bridge *jumping* up:

[Singing] Pretty, pretty moon a go fell down pon me,

What a pretty, pretty moon a go fell down pon me,

Pretty, pretty moon a go

fell down pon me,

What a pretty, pretty moon

a go fell down pon me.

She want pass, but she fraid

cause she realize say it was a

duppy. And she stand up and

she look. So she had on *big* pudding pan—shine! She

carrying fish into it. So she let down her basket. She

threw the fish into something, and she sail up the pud-

ding pan up in the air. And when the duppy see the

pudding pan coming down, him said, "Pretty, pretty

moon a fell down pon me," and just jump back down

into the water.

The Spirit of Stonehenge

S o you have moved from your old home; I was rather surprised to hear," I said to Ronald Dalton.

He nodded his head.

"We were very sorry to go, but nothing would have made us stay after what had happened. I know I did not tell you, but then we have not spoken of it more than is necessary, even to old friends."

We were sitting in the twilight of a June

evening. Outside the rain dripped from the trees, from the roof, from the windows; for there had been a dreadful thunderstorm.

"I would like to tell you what happened, if you care to listen," Ronald said abruptly.

I had been rather hoping he would, for he was a matter-of-fact man, and my curiosity had been stirred by the papers' accounts of the strange way one of their guests had committed suicide. So he started in his earnest way, which lent conviction to the story.

"My brother made great friends with Gavin Thomson in London. The first time I saw him was when he came to stay with us for a week. His great hobby was to dabble about in excavations, and, as his father had left him enough to live comfortably, he was able to indulge his taste.

"He was a good-looking boy, about twenty-nine, dark and manly. Though only young, he had made quite a name for himself already, even with the professors. There were tales of his living among the Bedouins, an unheard-of thing for a white man to do. But it was difficult to make him talk of his exploits.

"I took to him, as my brother had done; he had such a magnetic personality. He told us he had been reading up all the old books on Stonehenge which he could get hold of. The Druid theory fascinated him, and he was anxious to study some facts first-hand.

"He asked us if we had ever heard of ele-mentals; then laughed, and said we were not to be afraid that *he* was possessed by them. We asked him what the things were, for beneath his light manner I saw that he was really serious about them. He told us that they were a sort of ugly evil spirits, which had never had a form. Their one object was to find a human body in which to reside. They were supposed to have a certain power over human beings in places where great evil had prevailed.

"Quite abruptly he stopped, and began talking about the moon's rays on the dolmen at Stonehenge, and a peculiar theory he held, of which we understood nothing. I think he meant to puzzle us and make us forget.

"Now and then he descended to our level when he explained that the Druids were fond of conducting their ceremonies at certain times of the moon. 'That is why I have to do so much of my work at night,' he said. We had given him a latchkey so that he could come in when he liked. He told us that he was on the verge of a great discovery which would make history.

"After a fortnight's stay he left us to do some work in Brittany, but not before he had covered many sheets with writing. In three months he was back again. He looked gaunt and ill, and his eyes were sunken and bright with fever. We begged him to rest that night, but he would not hear of it, and when he spoke of Stonehenge his eyes gleamed in a strange manner.

"When he had gone out into the night I went up to his room to see if there was everything that he could want. There were books everywhere; one lay on the table, the place marked with something. I opened it at the place and a knife lay snugly between the pages.

It was curved, and of pure gold. I knew enough to know that it was a copy of a sacrificial knife; the edge was so sharp that I cut my finger rather badly.

"Curiosity aroused, I looked at the page, and this is what I read:

"'ELEMENTALS OF STONEHENGE. Though the day of the Druids is now long passed and the cries of their victims no longer haunt the night and the altar stone has ceased to drip blood, yet it is dangerous to go there when the sacrificial moon is full. For the Druids, by the blood they shed, their vile sacrifices and fellowship with the devil, attracted forces of evil to the place. So it is said that shapeless invisible horrors haunt the vicinity and at certain times crave a resting place in the human body. If once they enter in, it is only with great difficulty that they are evicted.'

"The book was many centuries old. I looked at the other books; they were all on the same subject. Gavin seemed to be quite crazy about it. I told my brother, and he said that he thought poor Gavin was overstrung.

" 'Perhaps he is possessed by an elemental,' he said, and we both laughed.

"Next night we resolved to follow him. When he went out as usual, the dog, to our surprise, jumped in the car. Gavin threw him out with a force that surprised us, and bade us call him back. We endeavoured to do so, but the animal seemed demented; he ran after the car like a mad thing, and both were soon lost in the distance.

"After half an hour we followed on the same road. It was a lovely night, warm, with the sky full of scudding clouds which every now and then hid the face of the moon and dimmed its light. Some little way off we left the car and started to walk across the grass. Tall and gaunt the dolmen stood out where the moonlight touched them. Somehow to me they looked unaccountably sinister, as if they longed to fall and crush one.

"We were still some way off when we saw a figure steal out from one of the great stones. In the dim light it looked like a misty wraith. I heard my brother draw in his breath sharply.

"It stopped before the altar stone, which was deeply in the shadow. Something flashed in the light—a knife; then it seemed from the stone itself came the most ear-splitting howl of agony.

"The moon went behind a cloud; we fled, stumbling over the wet grass, and in our haste missed the car. At last we found it, and, tumbling in, drove off at a great pace. When we got back again Gavin was already in bed and had come down to open the door. He was too tired to notice anything wrong, and we just said that we had been for a drive.

"Next day, after rather a sleepless night, we

were heartily ashamed of our weakness, and firmly resolved to follow Gavin again that night. All day he seemed very absorbed and dreamy, and talked only about the discovery that he was going to make.

"An hour after he left we were on his track. This time there was no moon, but we had an electric torch. I soon caught sight of Gavin; he was kneeling by the altar stone. It was reassuring to see his tweed-clad figure. We came up right behind, but he did not turn his head. Then I put my hand on his shoulder, but he did not move. He was unconscious. I raised his head and the light fell on glazed eyes, for he was dead. We laid him out on the altar stone seeking for a spark of life, but all in vain. There was blood on his shirt and the hilt of a little knife stuck out. There he lay on the sacrificial stone with hair disheveled, white upturned face and glassy eyes, while above towered the great stones, seeming to rejoice that once again homage had been paid by a sacrifice of blood. Queer shadows danced in the light of the lamp which my brother held in shaking hands.

"We stood with bowed heads in the presence of those great monuments; tombstones that would have done honour to a king. Then we gathered courage and took the body to the car. And Stonehenge let us go, content that once again its stones were wet with blood.

"It was an unconsidered thing we did, in that, and it might have led us into trouble; but we found a letter written by Gavin and his will which he had made, so we were freed from all blame or share in the matter.

"He said that the first few nights of his excavations at Stonehenge he had been unassailed and in a perfectly normal state of mind. Then a strange change came over him, so that at times he almost seemed to have lived there years before and to know all manner of secrets.

"Then it was that the desire to do the most dreadful things came over him. He questioned if he were mad or if it was the spirit of Stonehenge demanding a victim. The idea of elementals occurred to him, for he had been reading much about them of late.

"At last he tore himself away and went to Brittany to bury himself in work. But Stonehenge called him back, and he seemed to loose all power over himself. At last, after many sleepless nights, he came back, as he had known that he must.

"Then, one night he had seen a dog lying on the alter stone, and an irresistible desire to kill overpowered him. After the blood was shed he felt a strange joy and deep contentment, but something told him that he was being watched, so he took the body and ran to the car. He had discovered a short cut across the grass which cut off many miles, so that was how he got home before us.

"Next morning he awoke with the blood lust strong within him; he felt that if anything would come upon him at the Stones he must kill. All day he fought it. At times he would be filled with disgust at his thoughts, then fall to devising a plot to lure us to our fate.

"When we had mentioned our coming, a cold fear had seized him, but his words died in his throat when he tried to warn us. Then all the good that was in him seemed to make one last stand. He knew there was one way out—to offer a sacrifice of blood, and the victim to be himself.

"So that night he had offered his life as a propitiation for evil in the hope that he would regain the soul that once was his. He ended by begging us to forgive and forget.

"The letter accomplished a purpose. 'Suicide while of unsound mind,' was brought in. Suspicion was lifted from us, but afterwards Bob and I went away from the horrible place."

No one spoke. We sat in dead silence when he had finished. Then the gong rang, and we arose and knocked the ashes from our pipes.

The Moon

The moon like a flower

In heaven's high bower,

With silent delight

Sits and smiles on the night.

Rosicrucian Moon Initiation

hat takes place secretly in the Temple is shown openly in the heavens. As the moon gathers light from the Sun during her passage from the new to the full, so the man who treads the path of holiness by use of his golden opportunities in the East Room of selfless service gathers the material wherewith to make his luminous "wedding garment," and that material is best amalgamated on the night of the full moon. But conversely, as the moon gradually dissipates the accumulated light and draws nearer the Sun in order to make a fresh start upon a new cycle at the time of the new moon, so also according to the law of analogy those who have gathered their treasures and laid them up in heaven by service are at a certain time of the month closer to their Source and their Maker, their Father Fire in the higher spheres, than at any other time. As the great saviors of mankind are born at the winter solstice on the longest and darkness night of

the year, so also the process of Initiation which brings to birth in the invisible world one of the lesser saviors, *the Invisible Helper, is* most easily accomplished on the longest and darkest night of the month, that is to say, on the night of the new moon when the lunar orb is in the westernmost part of the heavens.

Erica Jong

Dearest
Man-in-the-Moon

Ever since our lunch of cheese

& moonjuice

on the far side of the sun,

I have walked the craters of New York,

a trail of slime

ribboning between my legs,

a phosphorescent banner

which is tied to you,

a beam of moonlight

focussed on your navel,

a silver chain

from which my body dangles,

& my whole torso chiming

like sleighbells in a Russian novel.

Dearest man-in-the-moon,

I used to fear moonlight

thinking her my mother.

I used to dread nights

when the moon was full.

I used to scream

"Pull down the shade!"

because the moonface leered at me,

because I felt her mocking,

because my fear lived in me

like rats in a wheel of cheese.

You have eaten out my fear.

You have licked

the creamy inside of my moon.

You have kissed

the final crescent of my heart

& made it full.

The Lunar Tides

Danger stalks on such nights, the moon is
dangerous:
Why will you walk beneath the
compelling luster
That draws the blood from your unwilling body?
The vampire moon with yellow streams of light
Drains the dim waters, sucks the moist air dry,
Casts cloudy spectres on the window pane—
The dead arise and walk again.

Oh, love, how are we drawn

Into this moon, this face as cold,

Remorseless as ambition, chilled with fever,

Burning with war that on these lunar tides

Draws all life to its danger; beautiful

It mocks the living glory of the sun;

Such golden, flowing motion, dipping in perilous play

Forgets the warm assurances of day.

Resistance dies, is plucked so gently from

Our paralyzed wills, we hardly know it gone.

We are surrendered to the moon:

The light compels us, pole-stars to its orbit,

We shine in darkness fixed, invisible.

Too late for the last withdrawal, we are lost

In the intricacies of yellow frost.

Fantasies in the brain, restlessness in the heart,

Desire for the unattainable, the pure romantic longing—

Ruined towers in the air, a yearning toward the sea,

For its deep death, so cool, and languorous:

These are the favorite symptoms written down;

The pressure of the moon on the rare spirit,

The wild attraction and the deep repulsion,

The irresistible compulsion.

The Monkeys
and the Moon

In long-past times there lived a band of monkeys
in a forest. As they rambled about they saw the
reflection of the moon in a well, and the leader
of the band said: "O friends, the moon has fallen into
the well. The world is now without a moon. Ought not
we to draw it out?"

The monkeys said, "Good; we will draw it out."

So they began to hold counsel as to how they
were to draw it out. Some of them said, "Do not you

know? The monkeys must form a chain, and so draw the moon out."

So they formed a chain, the first monkey hanging on to the branch of a tree, and the second to the first monkey's tail, and a third one in its turn to the tail of the second one. When in this way they were all hanging on to one another, the branch began to bend a good deal. The water became troubled, the reflection of the moon disappeared, the branch broke, and all the monkeys fell into the well and were disagreeably damaged.

A deity uttered this verse: "When the foolish have a foolish leader they all go to ruin like the monkeys which wanted to draw the moon up from the well."

Poke-
O'-Moonshine

One of our few satisfying mountain names is Poke-o'-moonshine, or Peekamoonshine, in the Adirondacks, the rule having been to burden our hills with a nomenclature either foolish or commonplace. In this lonely height is a cave with a crack in the roof through which, in certain phases of the moon, a ray of light will enter; and this peek or peep or poke of moonshine has given a name to the mountain itself. In 1757 a young

Huguenot noble, François du Bois, came to America
to join his regiment in Canada. He came the more
willingly because he knew that his sweetheart,
Clemence La Moille, would presently follow him, for
her father had incurred the dislike of certain political
enemies and had been virtually banished from the
kingdom. And, true enough, it was not long ere Emil
Le Moille and his daughter left their home, forever.
From New Rochelle, where they lived for a little time,
they went northward with an Indian guide and even-
tually settled in a lovely valley, east of Lake Champlain, on the bank of that river now called La Moille.
Clemence found a way to let her lover know their
whereabouts. He ascended the lake at the time with
Montcalm's force, which some days later attacked the
English near Lake George, and no doubt he cast a

longing eye at the peaceful hills that walled Champlain on its eastern side, for somewhere among them his lady awaited him.

Possibly he did not then imagine that in a few days he should be seeking her, a disgraced and heart-sick soldier, but so it fell out. Truth is, he had

little stomach for his business. He was less in love with war than with Clemence; being Protestant, he could not sympathize heartily with the scheme of a Catholic government against a Protestant people; and especially he loathed the brutalities that the Indians committed under permission of his fellow-officers. The horrible massacre that followed the French victory on Lake George ended his endurance. He stole away from camp at night, found a canoe, and in a few days he had reached the La Moille cabin, weak, discouraged, but with no jot of his love abated. He did not dare to meet the father. Exile though he was, the old man still revered his France and love his old profession of arms. When he learned that this proposed son-in-law was a deserter he would spurn him indignantly from his presence.

But with the girl it was otherwise. Du Bois gained audience with her, and with pity for his mental and bodily suffering mingled with her love she sheltered him. The French army would soon be returning toward the St. Lawrence, and he might be seen, chased, captured, and imprisoned, if not shot. Clemence lived almost as free a life as an Indian, and she was a wilful girl withal. It was an easy matter to absent herself for a day or two from home. In a night journey across the lake the young couple reached a trail leading into the fastnesses of the Adirondacks, and there Clemence left François, after directing him how he should reach Poke-o'-Moonshine, and promising to join him as soon as she could replenish their ammunition and recover some of her belongings.

A few days later she kissed her father and said she was going upon the lake. She never returned. Her dog reached home that evening with a letter in his collar, but rain or dew had made it illegible. Years afterward old La Moille, while hunting in the mountains, took shelter from the storm in the grotto of Poke-o'-Moonshine. The tempest lasted so long that he gave up the thought of leaving it that night, so he made himself comfortable and went to sleep. In the small hours he awoke to see a slender ray of moonlight falling through a chink in the rock. It rested on a scrap of gold lace from a military coat, and on a necklace—his daughter's. Was he dreaming? He reached out and took the pearls into his hand. They were real. Had the cave become the tomb of the young pair? Had they fallen victim to bears or panthers? It will never be known. But the cross that stood at the cave door for years after has banned all shadows, and the figures that glide over Lake Onewaska by moonlight are said to be François and Clemence.

Charles Baudelaire

The Sadness of
of the Moon

The Moon more indolently dreams tonight

Than a fair woman on her couch at rest,

Caressing, with a hand distraught and light,

Before she sleeps, the contour of her breast.

Upon her silken avalanche of down,

Dying she breathes a long and swooning sigh;

And watches the white visions past her flown,

Which rise like blossoms to the azure sky.

And when, at times, wrapped in her languor deep,

Earthward she lets a furtive tear-drop flow,

Some pious poet, enemy of sleep,

Takes in his hollow hand the tear of snow

Whence gleams of iris and of opal start,

And hides it from the Sun, deep in his heart.

—*Translated by F. P. Trurm*

The Crazed
Moon

C razed through much child-bearing

The moon is staggering in the sky;

Moon-struck by the despairing

Glances of her wandering eye

We grope, and grope in vain,

For children born of her pain.

Children dazed or dead!

When she in all her virginal pride

First trod on the mountain's head

What stir ran through the countryside

Where every foot obeyed her glance!

What manhood led the dance!

Fly-catchers of the moon,

Our hands are blenched, our fingers seem

But slender needles of bone;

Blenched by that malicious dream

They are spread wide that each

May rend what comes in reach.

Anonymous

The Man in the Moon

The Man in the Moon was caught in a trap

For stealing the thorns from another

man's gap.

If he had gone by, and let the thorns lie,

He'd never been Man in the Moon so high

The Terror by Night (*Fragment*)

ALCETAS:

Hear me, Melissus; I will tell you a dream

I had last night, which comes to mind again,

Now that I see the moon. I stood at the window

Which looks out on the field, and turned my eyes

Up to the sky: and then, all of a sudden,

The moon was loosened; and it seemed to me

That coming near and nearer as it fell down,

The bigger it appeared, until it tumbled

In the middle of the field, with a crash, and was

As big as a water-pot, and it spewed forth

A cloud of sparks, which spluttered, just as loud

As when you put a live coal under water

Till it goes out. For it was in that way

The moon, I'm telling you, in the middle of the field,

Went out, and little by little it all turned black.

And round about the grass went up in smoke.

And then, looking up at the sky, I saw was left

A kind of glimmer, or mark, or rather a hole,

From which it had been torn, and at that sight

I froze with terror; and don't feel easy yet.

MELISSUS:

And well you might, indeed; for sure enough,

The moon might tumble down into your field.

ALCETAS:

Who knows? For don't we often see in summer

Stars falling?

MELISSUS:

But then, there are so many stars:

And little harm if one or other of them

Do fall—there's thousands left. But there is only

This one moon in the sky, and nobody

Has ever seen it fall, except in dreams. . . .

—*Translated by John Heath-Stubbs*

Simples

O BELLA, BIONDA
SEI COME L'ONDA

Of cool sweet dew and

  radiance mild

The moon a web of silence weaves

In the still garden where a child

Gathers the simple salad leaves.

A moon-dew stars her hanging hair,

And moonlight touches her young brow;

And, gathering, she sings an air:

"Fair as the wave is, fair art thou."

Be mine, I pray, a waxen ear

To shield me from her childish croon;

And mine a shielded heart to her

Who gathers simples of the moon.

John Milton

Moon and Earth

Look downward on that globe, whose hither side

With light from hence, though but reflected,
shines:

That is Earth, the seat of Man; that light

His day, which else, as th'other hemisphere,

Night would invade; but there the neighbouring Moon

(So call that opposite fair star) her aid

Timely interposes; and, her monthly round

Still ending, still renewing, through mid-heaven,

With borrowed light her countenance triform

Hence fills and empties, to enlighten the Earth.

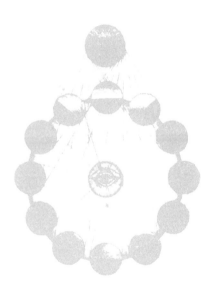

Why the Moon and Stars Receive Their Light from the Sun

Once upon a time there was great scarcity of food in the land. Father Anansi and his son, Kweku Tsin, being very hungry, set out one morning to hunt in the forest. In a short time Kweku Tsin was fortunate enough to kill a fine deer—which he carried to his father at their resting-place. Anansi was very glad to see such a supply of food, and requested his son to remain there on guard, while he went for a large basket in which to carry it home. An hour or so passed without his return, and Kweku Tsin became anxious. Fearing lest his father had lost his way, he called out loudly, "Father, father!" to guide him to the spot. To his joy he heard a voice reply, "Yes, my son," and immediately he shouted again, thinking it was Anansi. Instead of the latter, however, a terrible dragon appeared. This monster breathed fire from his great nostrils, and was altogether a dreadful sight to behold. Kweku Tsin was terrified at his approach and speedily hid himself in a cave nearby.

The dragon arrived at the resting-place, and was much annoyed to find only the deer's body. He vented his anger in blows upon the latter and went away. Soon after, Father Anansi made his appearance.

He was greatly interested in his son's tale, and wished to see the dragon for himself. He soon had his desire, for the monster, smelling human flesh, hastily returned to the spot and seized them both. They were carried off by him to his castle, where they found many other unfortunate creatures also awaiting their fate. All were left in charge of the dragon's servant— a fine, white cock—which always crowed to summon his master, if anything unusual happened in the latter's absence. The dragon then went off in search of more prey.

Kweku Tsin now summoned all his fellow-prisoners together, to arrange a way of escape. All feared to run away—because of the wonderful powers of the monster. His eyesight was so keen that he could detect a fly moving miles away. Not only that, but he could move over the ground so swiftly that none could outdistance him. Kweku Tsin, however, being exceedingly clever, soon thought of a plan.

Knowing that the white cock would not crow as long as he had grains of rice to pick up, Kweku scattered on the ground the contents of forty bags of grain—which were stored in the great hall. While the cock was thus busily engaged, Kweku Tsin ordered the spinners to spin fine hempen ropes, to make a strong ladder. One end of this he intended to throw up to heaven, trusting that the gods would catch it and hold it fast, while he and his fellow-prisoners mounted.

While the ladder was being made, the men killed and ate all the cattle they needed—reserving the bones for Kweku Tsin at his express desire. When all was ready the young man gathered the bones into a great sack. He also procured the dragon's fiddle and placed it by his side.

Everything was now ready. Kweku Tsin threw one end of the ladder up to the sky. It was caught and held. The dragon's victims began to mount, one after the other, Kweku remaining at the bottom.

By this time, however, the monster's powerful eyesight showed him that something unusual was happening at his abode. He hastened his return. On seeing his approach, Kweku Tsin also mounted the

ladder—with the bag of bones on his back, and the fiddle under his arm. The dragon began to climb after him. Each time the monster came too near the young man threw him a bone, with which, being very hungry, he was obliged to descend to the ground to eat.

Kweku Tsin repeated this performance till all the bones were gone, by which time the people were safely up in the heavens. Then he mounted himself, as rapidly as possibly, stopping every now and then to play a tune on the wonderful fiddle. Each time he did this, the dragon had to return to earth, to dance—as he could not resist the magic music. When Kweku was quite close to the top, the dragon had very nearly reached him again. The brave youth bent down and cut the ladder away below his own feet. The dragon was dashed to the ground—but Kweku was pulled up into safety by the gods.

The latter were so pleased with his wisdom and bravery in giving freedom to his fellow-men, that they made him the sun—the source of all light and heat to the world. His father, Anansi, became the moon, and his friends the stars, Thereafter, it was Kweku Tsin's privilege to supply all these with light, each being dull and powerless without him.

—*William H. Barker and C. Sinclair*

Christina Rosetti

The Half Moon Shows a Face of Plaintive Sweetness

The half moon shows a face of plaintive

sweetness

    Ready and poised to wax or wane;

A fire of pale desire in incompleteness,

    Tending to pleasure or to pain:—

Lo, while we gaze she rolleth on in fleetness

    To perfect loss or perfect gain.

Half bitterness we know, we know half sweetness;

This world is all on wax, on wane:

When shall completeness round time's incompleteness,

Fulfilling joy, fulfilling pain?—

    Lo, while we ask, life rolleth on in

      fleetness

        To finished loss or finished

      gain.

I Gazed Upon the Cloudless Moon

I gazed upon the cloudless moon,
And loved her all the night,
Till morning came and radiant noon,
And I forgot her light—

No, not forget—eternally
Remains its memory dear;
But could the day seem dark to me
Because the night was fair?

The Sun, the Moon, the Wind and the Sky

Once upon a time when the world was young, the Sun, the Moon and the Wind went to dine with their uncle and aunt, Thunder and Lightning. Their mother, the Sky, blessed them, and wishing them a merry party, waited alone for their return.

Now, both the Sun and the Wind were very greedy and selfish little boys. They ate all the sumptuous food that was given to them by their uncle and aunt, without any thought of their poor hungry mother who was sitting at home praying that they would be happy and enjoy themselves at the party. The gentle little Moon alone did not forget her mother. Of every dainty dish that was put before her she kept a little to take away to her mother.

"Well, children, what have you brought for me?" said the mother of the Sun, the Moon and the Wind, when they returned home at night.

"What do you mean, woman?" asked the Sun, who was her eldest child, insolently. "What do you expect me to bring for you? I went to dinner to eat and enjoy myself, not on an errand to bring food for you. Besides, you could not appreciate such delicacies as we were given, with your coarse ways of eating."

"Quite," echoed the little brat Wind, "you

don't know how to eat, nor can you, because you have no teeth in your mouth! And how can you expect us to spoil our fashionable clothes by stuffing our pockets up with food for you? Moreover, it is rude to fill our hankies with food. It is not done in the best circles. But how should a peasant know the price of jewels? What should you know of manners, good or bad?"

"Don't be so rude, brutes," interrupted the docile Moon, "it seems you don't know manners, talking to your mother like that!" Then, consoling the old woman she said: "Mother, taste this dinner I have brought for you. It is a little of everything we were given."

"May you live long, my moon child," said the old woman. And she turned indignantly to her sons: "The curses of Heaven shall fall on your two heads. You my eldest, you went out to feast and never thought of your old mother, although she slaves for you all day, you shall roast in eternal fire; your rays shall be scorching hot and shall burn all they touch, and men shall hate you when you appear in your pride! . . . . . . And you, my little scamp Wind, you who are so greedy and selfish, you will always blow in dry weather and shall parch or shrivel all that you touch, and men shall detest you when you are about! . . . . . . And you, my sweet daughter, you who thought of your mother, you shall flourish always; you shall be cool, calm, soft and beautiful; men shall be full of love when they see you; and they shall sing to you and call you blessed."

That is why the Sun is hated when it shines too hotly; the Wind despised when it blows strongly; and the Moon so loved by all.

—*Mulk Raj Anand*

The First
Eclipse

Once upon a time, long, long ago, before the Sun gave light to the day and the Moon illumined the night, there lived two sisters, Athit and Chan. They were served by a little slave-girl who waited on them always and did their bidding.

Now, one day, when it was festival time and it was the duty of all mankind to go to the great temple and pray, the two sisters and the little slave-girl arrived at the temple only to find that they had left behind them their rice bowl and the great wooden spoon they used for stirring the rice.

Athit and Chan told the little slave-girl to hurry back home to get them. This she did, but in her haste she forgot to get the great wooden spoon, returning to the sisters with the rice bowl only.

Athit took the rice bowl and demanded angrily of the girl what she had done with the wooden spoon.

"Alas, mistress," answered the little slave-girl, nervously, "alas, in my haste, I forgot it."

"Foolish girl!" Athit cried angrily. "Go back to the house at once and fetch it. And hurry!"

The little slave-girl ran off, her heart beating fast. She got the great wooden spoon and hurried back to her mistresses, Athit and Chan, without a moment's delay.

Meanwhile all mankind had assembled at the temple to pray and Athit and Chan waited impatiently for the return of the little slave-girl.

She came running back, handed Athit the great wooden spoon and stood respectfully before her mistress. And as she dutifully stood there, the angry Athit raised the great wooden spoon and hit her in the face. Before the little slave-girl had time to collect her thoughts Chan took hold of the spoon and hit her another great blow in the face.

The little slave-girl stood there in the presence of all mankind who were assembled for their prayers and her heart raged with anger that the two sisters should so have shamed her before all the people.

And as all the people knelt on the temple floor in prayer, the little slave-girl prayed too. But she prayed that when they were born again Athit and Chan should be shamed before all the world as she had been shamed by them.

And so it came about.

The years passed and the time came for Athit and Chan and the little slave-girl to die and be born again. Athit was reborn as the Sun and Chan was reborn as the Moon whose task it is to be ever on the move, travelling eternally at regular intervals of time. They are constantly being chased by an invisible being known as Rahu (this is the little slave-girl in her new life) who is bound by no such regular time-table. When she catches up with the Sun or the Moon she strikes them in the face in the presence of the whole world, to shame them as she was shamed by them. If she strikes them full in the face, there is a total eclipse, if she manages only a glancing blow there is a partial eclipse.

Mankind has now become accustomed to the light of the Sun and the Moon, and when Rahu strikes them the people fear she may put out their light forever. At the very first sign of an eclipse, therefore, the people bring out their drums and their gongs and musical instruments of all kinds and beat them and strike them and play them and shout and make such a din as to frighten Rahu away. Then the

Sun or the Moon regains its brightness and continues on its eternal journey until Rahu turns up once more to strike them in the face.

Thus does Rahu, formerly a poor little slave-girl, who was humiliated before all mankind by her foolish mistresses, now strike terror in the hearts of men.

And that is the story behind the first eclipse.

Welcome to
the Moon

Welcome, precious stone of night,

Delight of the skies, precious stone

of the night,

Mother of stars, precious stone of the night,

Child reared by the sun, precious stone of the night,

Excellency of stars, precious stone of the night.

Medicine
Formula

When the new moon appears it is shouted to:

I shall prosper,

I shall yet remain alive.

Even if people do say of me,

"Would that he died!"

Just like thee shall I do,

Again shall I arise.

Even if all sorts of evil beings

devour thee,

When frogs eat thee up,

Many evil beings—lizards,

Even when those eat thee up,

Still dost thou rise
again.
Just like you will I do
in time to come.
Bo!

—Translated by Edward Sapir

The Moon and the Yew Tree

This is the light of the mind, cold and planetary.

The trees of the mind are black. The light is blue.

The grasses unload their griefs on my feet as if I were God,

Prickling my ankles and murmuring of their humility.

Fumey, spirituous mists inhabit this place

Separated from my house by a row of headstones.

I simply cannot see where there is to get to.

The moon is no door. It is a face in its own right,

White as a knuckle and terribly upset.

It drags the sea after it like a dark crime; it is quiet

With the O-gape of complete despair. I live here.

Twice on Sunday, the bells startle the sky—

Eight great tongues affirming the Resurrection.

At the end, they soberly bong out their names.

The Yew tree points up.

It has a Gothic shape.

The eyes lift after it

and find the moon.

The moon is my mother.

She is not sweet like Mary.

Her blue garments unloose small bats and owls.

How I would like to believe in tenderness—

The face of the effigy, gentled by candles,

Bending, on me in particular, its mild eyes.

I have fallen a long way. Clouds are flowering

Blue and mystical over the face of the stars.

Inside the church, the saints will be all blue,

Floating on their delicate feet over the cold pews,

Their hands and faces stiff with holiness.

The moon sees nothing of this. She is bald and wild.

And the message of the yew tree is blackness—blackness

        and silence.

Madman's Song

Better to see your cheek grown hollow,

Better to see your temple worn,

Than to forget to follow, follow,

After the sound of a silver horn.

Better to bind your brow with willow

And follow, follow until you die,

Then to sleep with your head on a golden pillow,

Nor lift it up when the hunt goes by.

Better to see your cheek grown

  sallow,

And your hair grown

  gray, so soon, so soon,

Than to forget to hallo,

  hallo,

After the milk-white hounds of the moon.

Illustrations

Page 2 — Assyrian Moon Tree guarded by unicorns.

Page 5 — The Sacred Stone of the Moon Goddess, from *Religions de l'Antiquité*, 1825.

Page 8 —19th-century lunar astronomy sketch by Camille Flammarion, 1881

Page 15 — The lunar horoscope.

Page 18 — Coin of Megarus illustrating the movement or journey of the moon, from *The Migration of Symbols*, 1894.

Page 20 — The Moon Deity in Triune form. Three little altars are shown side by side representing the waxing moon, the full moon, and waning moon. From *Sur la Culte de Mithra*, 1847.

Page 32 — The Moon Swastika from a coin of Crete. This is a "four-armed" or square swastika such as is usually associated with the sun's movement, but here the disc of the sun is replaced by the lunar crescent. From *The Migration of Symbols*, Goblet d'Alviella, the Constable Company, 1894.

Page 41 — Moon insect, 1847.

Page 58 — Sinn, the moon god enshrined by the circle of the full moon, from *Sur la Culte de Mithra*, 1847.

Page 68 — Sinn receiving a worshipper brought to him, from *Ancient Pagan and Modern Christian Symbolism*, 1876.

Page 74 — The French lampoon journal, *La Lune*, 1879.

Page 77 — The moon, from an 1831 manuscript.

Page 84 — The moon's influence, from a 16th-century engraving.

Page 94 — Assyrian Moon Tree in the form of a pillar, guarded by winged monsters, from *Sur la Culte de Mithra*, 1847.

Page 97 — Sinn enthroned, holding the moon as his emblem. The two hounds, one coming and one going, represent the waxing and waning moon. From *Sur la Culte de Mithra*, 1847.

Page 100 — Moon hemisphere by Johannis Hevelius, 1647.

Page 103 — The Sacred Stone of the Moon Goddess, enshrined in her temple, from *Religions de l'Antiquité*, 1825.

Page 106 — Mesopotamian coin entitled "Hecate Triformis." From *The Migration of Symbols*, 1894.

Page 111 — The moon god seated in a crescent boat, paddling himself across the sky. Our hero is shown fighting a lion and a unicorn, who threaten to devour the moon. From Ur, 2300 B.C.

Page 113 — The Sacred Phoenician Moon Tree guarded by winged lions. From the *Migration of Symbols*, 1894.

Page 116 — Moon icon from *La Fonderie Typographique Francaise*.

Page 119 — Moon Crater, 1878, artist unknown.

Page 121 — The phase of the moon, by Jacques Devaulx, 1583.

Page 126 — Assyrian Moon Tree with Unicorn and Winged Lion. From *Sur la Culte de Mithra*, 1847.

Page 130 — The Gateway of the Shrine of Venus at Paphos. From *Religions de l'Antiquité*, 1825.

Page 138 — Moon icon from *La Fonderie Typographique Francaise*.

Page 144 — Sinn enthroned on the crescent. Before him is the morning star, Istar, who in later centuries will replace him as chief deity of the moon. From *Sur la Culte de Mithra*, 1847.

Page 146 — Emblem of Isis, date unknown.

Page 149 — Moon Swastika from Sicilian coins. The cycle of the moon and its journey across the sky are represented in the swastika. From *Symbolical Language of Ancient Art and Mythology*, 1892.

Biographies

The Bushmen of South Africa's 19th-century *Prayer to the Moon* is typical of their obsession with lunar deities.

Armand Schwerner's working of this *Anonymous Alsean Poem* was first published in the collection *Shaking the Pumpkin*.

Italo Calvino routinely defied the limits of realism by delving into fantasy and myth, as in this excerpt from *Cosmicomics*.

Religion and folklore mingle in *Marcu Beza's* translations of Romanian incantations. Beza lectured at King's College for many years.

Wolfgang Amadeus Mozart's The Magic Flute made a big splash in 1791. People were astonished by his tragic, well-drawn characters.

Born in Essex in 1923, *Denise Levertov* authored more than a dozen volumes of poetry and lectured at Stanford and Tufts.

Sasha Fenton is well known for her studies of moon astrology. In addition to a regular astrology column, she has published six books on this subject.

A large number of *African Folktales* are obsessed with tales of lunar creation and influence.

English lexicographer, essayist, poet, and moralist *Samuel Johnson* published *A Journey to the Western Islands of Scotland* in 1775.

The Amazonian *Creation of the Moon* can be found in *Selected Translations*. Merwin is the recipient of numerous literary awards; he currently lives in Hawaii.

These anonymous Haiku are thought to date to the 5th century.

The Pennsylvania Dutch carefully cultivated their agriculture according to lunar cycles, a continuation of earlier European practices. *Moon Gardening* is a classic example.

French poet *Paul Verlaine* published several volumes of poetry in the 1860s; his best known work is *Clair de Lune* (1866).

The *Nursery Rhyme Moon, Moon* can be found in American folklore and dates from the 1700s.

This *Jamaican Folklore* tale can be found in Daryl Dance's *Folklore from Contemporary Jamaica*.

The moon is oft-associated with Stonehenge, as in this early-20th-century tale from English critic *Jasper John*.

William Blake is today deemed an apocalyptic visionary poet and artist. During his own age, however, he was considered insane.

Max Heindel, a Rosicrucian mystic, penned this passage in his 1920 tome, *Ancient and Modern Initiation*.

Erica Jong is best known for her novel, *Fear of Flying*, but has also published five volumes of poetry.

Marya Zaturenska was born in 1902. This poem is from her collection *Cold Morning Sky*.

In this *Tibetan Tale*, the resemblances to Aesop are conspicuous.

The American legend *Poke-O'-Moonshine* dates to the 19th-century.

Charles Baudelaire's Les Fleurs du mal (1857) is considered one of the masterpieces of French verse.

W. B. Yeats was born in Dublin in 1865. He received the Nobel Prize for literature in 1923.

The origin of the *Man in the Moon* is unknown.

Giacomo Leopardi was considered the greatest Italian Romantic poet of his era (1830s.)

James Joyce is well known for his great novels (*Ulysses*, *Finnegans Wake*), but he also published several of small volumes of verse.

John Milton was the greatest poet of his age. To this day, his *Paradise Lost* is considered a classic for the ages.

In this charming *West African Folktale*, Kweku Tsin displays the cleverness of Odysseus combined with the talents of Orpheus.

Christina Rosetti's work ranges from fantasy and ballads to sonnets and religious poetry.

Emily Brontë, one of the famous Brontë sisters, was responsible for the masterpiece *Wuthering Heights*.

Lunar influence is predominant in many *Indian Fairytale*s. This one is thought to date from the 19th century.

The allure and mystery surrounding lunar eclipses account for a huge number of *Thai Legends*, including this one.

This *Anonymous Gaelic Poem* dates to the 1700s.

The healing powers of the moon are greatly admired in this *Takelma Indian* litany.

Sylvia Plath's first volume of poetry, *The Colossus*, appeared in 1960, followed by her famous novel, *The Bell Jar*, in 1963. Less than a month later, she committed suicide in London.

American poet *Elinor Wylie's Collected Poems* was published in 1932. She aroused both adoration and disdain; the latter came predominantly from Virginia Woolf.

Acknowledgments

"Dearest Man in the Moon" from *Loveroot* by Erica Jong. © 1968, 1969, 1973, 1974, 1975 by Erica Mann Jong. Reprinted by permission of Henry Holt and Co., Inc.

"The Lunar Tides" from *Collected Poems of Marya Zaturenska* © 1937 by Marya Zaturenska Gregory. Reprinted by permission of Viking Penguin, a division of Penguin Books USA Inc.

Excerpt from *Masks of God: Primitive Mythology* by Joseph Campbell © 1959, 1969, renewed 1987 by Joseph Campbell. Reprinted by permission of Viking Penguin, a division of Penguin Books USA Inc.

"Madman's Song" from *Collected Poems by Elinor Wylie* © 1921 by Alfred A. Knopf Inc. and renewed 1949 by William Rose Benet. Reprinted by permission of the publisher.

"The Moon Eclipse Exorcism" from *Shaking the Pumpkin* by Jerome Rothenberg. © 1972 by Jerome Rothenberg. Reprinted by permission of Sterling Lord Literistic, Inc.

"The Moon and the Yew Tree" from *The Collected Poems of Sylvia Plath* edited by Ted Hughes. © 1963 by the Estate of Sylvia Plath. Reprinted by permission of HarperCollins Publishers, Inc.

"The Creation of the Moon" from *Selected Translations 1948-1968* by W. S. Merwin. © translation 1968 by W. S. Merwin. Reprinted by permission of Georges Borchardt, Inc.

"The Crazed Moon" from *The Poems of W.B. Yeats: A New Edition*, edited by Richard J. Finneran. © 1933 by Macmillan Publishing Company, renewed 1961 by Bertha Georgie Yeats. Reprinted by permission of Simon & Schuster.

"Pretty, Pretty Moon a Fell Down pon Me" from *Darly C. Dance's Folklore from Contemporary Jamaicans*. © 1985 by The University of Tennessee Press. Reprinted by permission of the University of Tennessee Press.

"The Distance of the Moon" from *Cosmicomics* by Italo Calvino © 1965 by Giulio Einaudi. English translation © 1968 by Harcourt Brace & Company and Jonathan Cape Ltd. Reprinted by permission of Harcourt Brace & Company.

Excerpt from *The Goddess of the Moon* by Sasha Fenton. © 1994 by Sasha Fenton. Reprinted by permission of HarperCollins.

"Secret Festival" and "September Moon" by Denise Levertov. © 1959 by Denise Levertov. Reprinted by permission of New Directions, Inc.